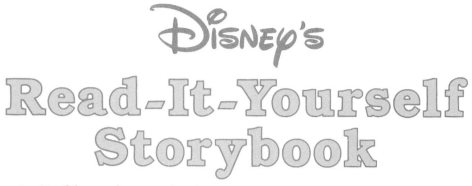

Disney's
Read-It-Yourself
Storybook

A Collection of Six Easy-to-Read Stories

A GOLDEN BOOK • NEW YORK
Western Publishing Company, Inc., Racine, Wisconsin 53404

Foreword

"Mom! Dad! Listen to me! I can read!" It's one of the most triumphant moments for any child—and any parent.

Now, of course, your new little reader wants to practice all the time. When children start reading, it takes time for their reading vocabulary to match their spoken vocabulary. They need books with easily recognizable words to encourage their sense of achievement. They need simple sentences, because they can't yet keep track of complicated thoughts on paper—even though they may speak and understand long, complex sentences. And finally, children also need some words they don't know already, to challenge them to further efforts. Stories with these elements draw children into reading independently.

Disney's Read-It-Yourself Storybook provides all these things. The vocabulary is carefully chosen and monitored to blend familiarity with challenge. Simple sentences, with a few complex ones mixed in, make reading easy and interesting for all children, whether they are getting ready to read, are beginning to read, or are already reading on their own.

Yet reading involves more than just words and sentences, and *Disney's Read-It-Yourself Storybook* is far more than that. Walt Disney's timeless characters and humorous situations come to life for children. They'll pick up this book over and over again to follow Mickey Mouse's adventures with his friends—on boats and bikes, around the neighborhood, and at the pet show. They'll laugh at Donald Duck's escapades in the toy store, and his plots to outwit Chip and Dale.

Lively, interesting characters and situations combined with ease of reading and a bit of challenge are irresistible to young readers. Your child will return to these stories until every word had been mastered—and after that, too, for the pleasure and comfort of familiar old friends. In the end, that's what *Disney's Read-It-Yourself Storybook* will become: a beloved old friend.

—Sally R. Bell
Reading Consultant

Table of Contents

Mickey Mouse
and the Peanuts

"Peanuts are magic,"
Mickey Mouse said to
Donald Duck.

"Come and take a walk
with me.
I will show you
what peanuts can do."

Mickey and Donald
went to see Goofy.
"I am so sad,"
said Goofy.
"I have nothing
to do."

"Here is something
to do," said Mickey.
"Put this peanut
on your nose."

Goofy put the peanut
on his nose.
He ran with the peanut
on his nose!

"Good for you!"
said Mickey.
"Good for me!"
said Goofy.
"I am happy now!"
"The peanut did it!"
said Mickey.

Mickey and Donald
went to see Minnie.
"Can you help me?"
she asked.
"My house is too quiet."

"This will help you,"
said Mickey.

He put peanuts
on the window.
"Peep! Peep! Peep!"
Birds came flying
to the window.

Bluebirds!
Redbirds!
Yellow birds, too!
"My house is not too
quiet now!" said Minnie.
"The peanuts did it!"
said Mickey.

Mickey and Donald
went to the park.
Daisy was there.

"Help! Help!"
she cried.
"My friend fell
into the water!"

"Where is your friend?"
asked Mickey.
"There she is!"
said Daisy.

"See that ladybug?"
said Daisy.
"You must save her!"

"This will save her!"
said Donald.
He took a nut
and made a boat!

"You did it!"
said Daisy.
"You saved my friend."
"The peanut did it!"
said Donald.

Pluto came by.
He barked and barked.
"Pluto wants to eat,"
said Mickey.

"It is time
to go home.
I will make
a big dinner."

Pluto barked
all the way home.
"I wish he would stop,"
said Donald.

"What is for dinner?"
asked Daisy.
"Wait and see,"
said Mickey.

"Woof! Woof! Woof!"
Pluto barked and barked.
"He will not stop,"
said Donald.

"Surpise!" said Mickey.
"Peanut butter!"
"I love peanut butter!"
said Daisy.

"I do, too!"
said Donald.
"Woof! Woof! Woof!"
barked Pluto.

They all ate.
They all ate
a lot of
peanut butter.

"Did you like
your dinner?"
asked Mickey.
"Yes!" said Donald.
"Yes!" said Daisy.
Pluto tried to bark.
He could not.
He could not
open his mouth.

"Hurray!" said Donald.
"Pluto has stopped
barking!"
"The peanut butter did it!"
said Mickey.
Pluto just smiled and smiled.

Donald Duck
at the Toy Store

Huey, Dewey, and Louie
were not happy.
"Why are you so sad?"
asked Donald.
"We have nothing to do,"
said Huey.

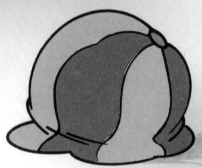

"Why don't you play?"
asked Donald.
"Why don't you play
with your toys?"
"We are tired of
the same old toys,"
said Dewey.
"Very, very tired," said Louie.

"We will go
to the toy store,"
said Donald.
"We will get
some new toys."
"Hurray!"
said Huey, Dewey,
and Louie.

"Here is a good toy.
Can we get this?"
asked Huey.

"I will try it
for you,"
said Donald.

"No, Uncle Donald!
Stop! Stop!
Do not jump.
Do not jump
in the store.
Watch out, Uncle Donald!"

SALE

"That toy is not good,"
said Donald.
"That toy is not good
for you."

"Here is a good toy,"
said Dewey.
"Can we get these skates?"

"I will try them,"
said Donald.

"No, Uncle Donald!
Stop! Stop!
Do not skate.
Do not skate
in the store.
Watch out, Uncle Donald!"

51

"Those skates are not good,"
said Donald.
"Those skates are not good
for you."

"Here is a good toy,"
said Louie.
"Can we get this
big, big balloon?"

"I will try it,"
said Donald.

"No, Uncle Donald!
Stop! Stop!
You must not play.
You must not play
in the store.
Watch out, Uncle Donald!"

"So many toys!"
said Donald.
"I will try this bike.
I will try these paints.
I will try lots of toys!"

"Stop, Mr. Duck!
Stop! Stop!"

"Not now,"
said Donald.
"I must try this car!
I must try this kite!"

"Your uncle must go,"
said the storekeeper.
"Can you make him
go now?"

"Uncle Donald,
we must go home,"
said Huey, Dewey, and Louie.
"We must go home now."
"Not now,"
said Donald.
"I must try this train!"

"Please, please!
Make him go!"
said the storekeeper.
"I will give you these toys
if you make him go."
"Hurray!"
said Huey, Dewey, and Louie.

"Look, Uncle Donald.
Look at our new toys!
You can play with these toys
at home!"
"No," said Donald.
"I am tired of toys.
Very, very tired."

Mickey Mouse
and His Boat

Mickey Mouse had a boat.
It was a little boat.
It had room for Mickey
and Pluto.

Mickey fished from his boat.
He watched the birds.
He talked to Pluto.

Mickey was happy.
He had his boat.
He had his dog.
What more did he need?

One day Morty and Ferdie
wanted to go fishing.

"But there is no room,"
said Mickey.
"There is no room
for Pluto."

Pluto watched the boat.
He barked and barked.
He wanted to go, too.

Mickey started to fish.
Morty and Ferdie
started to fish, too.

Something pulled at
Mickey's line.
"A fish!" he cried.
"Pull it in!" cried Ferdie.

Mickey pulled.
Mickey pulled Ferdie
into the water.

"There is no room,"
said Mickey.
"Next time only Pluto
will go."

But the next day
Minnie Mouse
wanted to go.
So did Clarabelle Cow.

"There is no room,"
said Mickey.
"There is a lot of room,"
said Clarabelle.

She sat down.
"See?" she said.
"I see," said Mickey.

They all got out
of the water.

"You need a bigger boat,"
said Minnie.
She took Mickey to
buy a boat.

Mickey bought a
big boat.
He gave his little boat
to Goofy.

The next day
Mickey went fishing.
Minnie and Clarabelle
went, too.
So did Pluto.

But the next day
Horace Horsecollar went.
So did Mr. Black.
Mr. Black had seven children.

"There is no room,"
said Mickey.
"There is a lot of room,"
said Mr. Black.

Pluto watched the boat.
He watched and watched.
He did not want to go.

Seven children tried
to play in the boat.
Seven children hopped.
Seven children jumped.

The boat turned over.
People came to help.
"You need a bigger boat,"
said a man.

"Yes," said Mr. Black.
"You could get
a very big boat.
Then people would pay
to ride in it."

"What a good idea,"
said Mickey.
Mickey bought
a very big boat.

A lot of people
went out on
Mickey's boat.

A lot of people
worked on the boat, too.

But Pluto stopped
going with Mickey.

One day Mickey saw Goofy.
Goofy was in his little boat.
Mickey saw Pluto.
Pluto was in
the little boat, too.

Mickey watched the little boat.

He watched and watched.

He wanted to fish.

He wanted to be with Pluto.

The next day Mickey sold
his very big boat.
He bought a small boat.

Mickey and Pluto went fishing.
Mickey did not catch any fish.
He did not care.
He had his boat.
He had his dog.
What more did he need?

Mickey Mouse
and the Bicycle Race

"A race!" said Mickey Mouse.
"We should have
a bike race."

Mickey and Goofy
got on a bike.
Donald and Daisy
got on another bike.

"One, two, three...
GO!"
said Minnie.
They were off!
Two bikes raced fast
down the hill.

"Stop! Stop!" said Goofy.
"Where is my
lucky penny?"
One bike stopped.

"Here it is!"
said Goofy.
"Now we can go."
They were off!
Two bikes raced fast.

"Stop! Stop!"
said Goofy.
"I have to eat.
I have to be strong
for the race."
One bike stopped.

"Now we can go,"
said Goofy.
They were off!
Two bikes raced fast.

"Stop! Stop!"
said Goofy.
"I must read my book.
I must read
about racing."
One bike stopped.

"Now we can go,"
said Goofy.
They were off!

"Faster!" said Mickey.
"We must catch up."
"I am going as fast
as I can," said Goofy.

Donald and Daisy
were still ahead.
"Do not give up,"
said Mickey.
"Never," said Goofy.

"We are next to them,"
said Mickey.
"We can win.
We can win the race!"

"Stop! Stop!"
said Goofy.
"No! No!"
said Mickey.
"Not now."

"Yes! Yes!"
said Goofy.
"Now.
Look at Ferdie.
He looks so sad."
One bike stopped.

"I lost my new kite,"
said Ferdie.
"I lost it
in that tree."

"We will get your kite,"
said Mickey.
Mickey and Goofy
got the kite.

Mickey and Goofy
got back on
the bike.

"I hope you win
the race," said Ferdie.

Mickey and Goofy
rode very fast.
But they could not
catch Daisy and Donald.

"We won!" said Donald.
"We won!" said Daisy.
Minnie gave them
each a prize.

Mickey and Goofy
smiled at Donald
and Daisy.
They began
to go.

"Stop! Stop!"
said Minnie.
"I have prizes
for you two.

"It is a prize
for being good friends
to Ferdie."
"We are winners, too!"
said Goofy.
"Yes, you are,"
said Minnie.

Then they all
took a ride
together.

Donald Duck
and the Garden

Donald Duck wanted
a garden.
He planted seeds.
"The seeds will grow,"
said Donald.
"They will grow into
good things to eat."

Chip and Dale came
to watch.
Chip and Dale liked
to eat seeds.

"Stop! Stop!"
said Donald.

"Help! Help!"
cried Chip.
"Run! Run!"
cried Dale.

133

"I know them,"
said Donald.
"I know them
very well.
They will be back.
I will be ready."

Chip and Dale
came back.
They wanted
to eat.

There was something new
in the garden.
Chip and Dale
did not care.
They began to eat.

"BOO!"
"Help! Help!"
cried Chip.
"Run! Run!"
cried Dale.

Chip and Dale
did not come back
for a long time.
The seeds grew.
They grew into
good things to eat.

But then Chip and Dale
came back.
Chip and Dale liked
good things to eat.

"Stop! Stop!"
cried Donald.
"Help! Help!"
cried Chip.
"Run! Run!"
cried Dale.

"We know Donald,"
said Chip.
"We know him
very well," said Dale.
"He will not
let us eat.
We must do something."

"We will go back
at night,"
said Chip.
"Donald will be
sleeping then."
That is what they did.

There was something new
in the garden.
Chip and Dale
did not care.
They began to eat.

POP!
"Help! Help!"
cried Chip.
"Run! Run!"
cried Dale.

"Ha! Ha!"
said Donald.
"They will not
come back.
But I will be ready
if they do."

Chip and Dale
came back.
"We will not run
this time,"
they said.

"Look!" said Chip.
"Someone is here.
Do we know him?"
"I do not think so,"
said Dale.

"THIS IS MY FOOD,"
said the someone.
"GO AWAY."
"Help! Help!"
cried Chip.
"Run! Run!"
cried Dale.

"Ha! Ha!"
said Donald.
"They will not
be back."

But Chip and Dale
came back.
They liked the
good things
in Donald's garden.

"They are back!"
said Donald.
"I will make them
go away."

"Help! Help!"
cried Chip.
"Run! Run!"
cried Dale.

"Ha! Ha!"
said Donald.
"They may come back.
But they will not
get in."

Donald worked hard.
He built a high fence.
He put something
on it.

Chip and Dale
came back.
"What is this?"
they cried.
"We can not get in."

"Look!" said Chip.
"Someone is coming.
Do we know him?"

"Oh, yes," said Dale.
"It is Goofy.
And here come
Daisy and Minnie
and others.
We know them all."

Chip and Dale watched.
All their friends
came to see Donald.
They came for a party—
a party with good things
to eat.

"Look! Look at all
the good things
to eat," said Chip.
"I wish we could
go to the party,"
said Dale.

Donald looked at
Chip and Dale.
"I did not want you
in my garden.
But I do want you
at my party.
Come in and have fun!"

Mickey Mouse
and the Pet Show

Mickey Mouse and Donald Duck
were taking a walk.
Pluto was with them.

They saw a man
putting up a sign.
The sign said,
"Bring your pet
to pet show today!"

"Pluto can be in the pet show!"
said Mickey.
"Yes," said Donald.
"But he needs a bath."

Pluto heard the word *bath*.
Pluto knew the word *bath*.
Pluto did not want a bath!
Pluto ran away.

Mickey ran after Pluto.
Donald ran after Mickey.
They ran up a street.

Pluto could not run away.
They all went to Mickey's house.

Mickey got out the tub.
Minnie put in the water.

Daisy got out the towels.
Goofy put in the soap.
Everything was ready.
But where was Pluto?

Everyone looked for Pluto.
They looked for a long time.
They could not find him.

"I am tired," said Mickey.
"I am going to sit down."

Mickey sat down.
"Bow-wow!" said the chair.
It was Pluto!

"Come on, Pluto.
You must have a bath!"
said Mickey.
Mickey put Pluto into the tub.

Pluto got all wet.
Mickey got all wet, too.
So did Minnie and Goofy
and Donald and Daisy!

Mickey washed Pluto with soap.
The soap made Pluto slide.

Pluto slid out of Mickey's hands.
He tried to run away again.

"Pluto, stop!
Do not go in my car!"
cried Mickey.
But Pluto jumped into the car.

Mickey ran to the car.

Pluto jumped out of the car.

Pluto saw Mickey's face.
He did not see
where he was going.

He did not see
the clothesline.
Crash!

"Come on, Pluto.
You must have a bath!"
said Mickey.

Oh, no!
Look at Mickey and Pluto!

Mickey put Pluto back
into the tub.
"Do not run away again!"
said Mickey.
"You must have a bath!"

Pluto knew he had to
have a bath.
He did not try
to run away again.
But he sang.

At last Pluto was ready.
"Put a bow on him,"
said Daisy.

Pluto did not want a bow.
"Hold on to him!"
cried Mickey.
"Hold on to him!"
cried Donald and Daisy.
"Put the bow on him!"
cried Goofy and Minnie.

Oh, no!
Look at Donald!

At last Pluto was ready.
He looked great!
Everyone walked to
the pet show.

They all saw the sign.
They saw *all* of the sign.
The sign said, "Bring your pet *cat*
to pet show today!"

"Pluto is not a *cat*!"
said Mickey.
"Pluto is a dog!
He can not be in
the pet show!"

BRING YOUR P
TO
PET
SHO
TO

But Pluto did not care.
He looked great!
He felt great!
He would not need
another bath
for a very long time!